Roble's Rain Dance

Paula Knight • Gavin Scott

BONNEY PRESS

Published by Bonney Press,
an imprint of Hinkler Books Pty Ltd
45–55 Fairchild Street
Heatherton Victoria 3202 Australia
www.hinkler.com.au

BONNEY
PRESS

© Hinkler Books Pty Ltd 2012

Author: Paula Knight
Illustrator: Gavin Scott
Prepress: Graphic Print Group

ISBN: 978 1 7430 8951 4

Printed and bound in China

Roble is hot and thirsty. It hasn't rained in his desert for a long time.

Roble shares a burrow with many other gerbils. During the day, it gives them shelter from the burning sun and hungry swooping eagles. Every gerbil has their very own entrance hole.

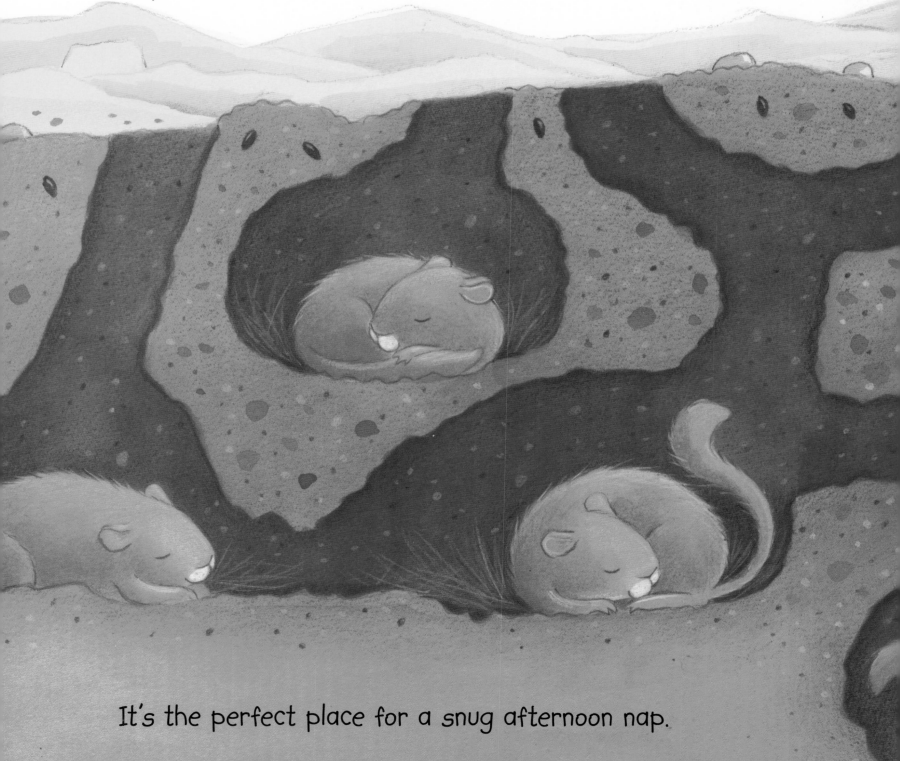

It's the perfect place for a snug afternoon nap.

At night, Roble searches for food. He bumps into Juba gerbil, who lives in the hole next door.

"Not much to eat tonight," says Juba. "Only curled-up crusty old cactus leaves!"

So they scurry to the next plant instead.

"Where are all the prickly pear fruits?" says Roble.

"What are we to do?" cries Juba.

They collect what scraps of food they can find, and Roble shares it with the other gerbils.

Up pops little Gogo.

"Thank you so much!" he says. "My tummy was rumbling!"

One by one, the gerbils poke their heads up to say thank you. But...

The gazelles ate all the aloe!
The prickly pear was all but bare!
The cactus is all crusty!

When Roble was a baby, they had plenty to eat. The grown-ups sang songs and danced around the fruitful bushes, while the young gerbils splished and splashed in cool muddy puddles.

"I've had an idea!" Roble says. "Let's meet at the date palm high on the hill near the sky!"

The gerbils march past the bare prickly pear, around the crusty cactus and the barren aloe...

...up the big hill over the dry dusty earth to the date palm at the top.

It's droopy!

They gaze up at the clear starry sky.

"Not a single fluffy cloud!" sighs Juba.

"What shall we do, Roble?" they ask.

"We must perform a rain dance for the sky by pittering and pattering our feet on the earth, like the sound of rain."

High on the hill where the sky can see them, the gerbils hold hands.

They begin to sing and dance.

"Rain, rain, come to stay,

Come to visit us today!

Rain, rain, fall and pour,

Sprinkle on the desert floor."

Pitter-patter, pitter-patter go their tiny feet.

"Rain, rain, pitter-patter,

Feed the cactus, make it fatter!

Rain, rain, and cloud-burst,

Shower us and quench our thirst."

Round and round they dance and chant until
they flop to the floor, exhausted.

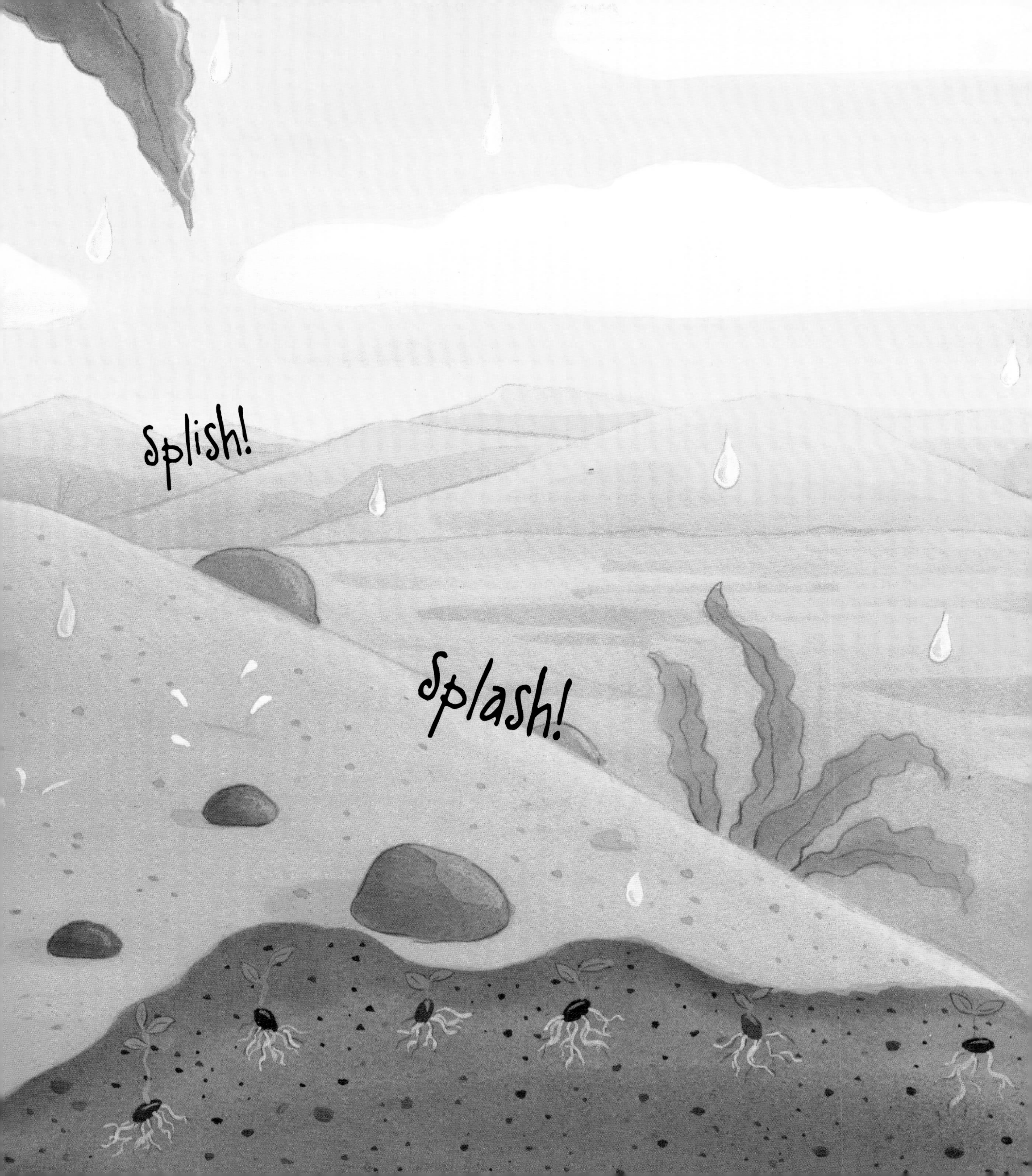
Splish!
Splash!

"Wake up!" cries Roble. "Our rain dance has worked!"

Later that day, beautiful flowers bloom all over the desert.

The gerbils are so happy that they want to reward Roble for helping to bring the rain. They celebrate by crowning him 'Rain King'.

There is enough for everybody to eat and drink, with plenty left over...

...for splishing and splashing in cool muddy puddles!

'Roble' is a Somali name meaning 'born during the rainy season'. Somalia is a country in East Africa.